D0577703

THE HAND-ME-DOWN HORSE

by
Marion Hess Pomeranc

illustrated by
Joanna Yardley

Albert Whitman & Company • Morton Grove, Illinois

The text typeface is Weidemann.

The illustrations were painted in
Linel watercolors, prisma color, pen & ink.

Designed by Lindaanne Donohoe.

Library of Congress Cataloging-in-Publication Data

Pomeranc, Marion Hess.
The hand-me-down horse/written by Marion Hess Pomeranc;
illustrated by Joanna Yardley.
p. cm.
Summary: Before she leaves for America, Aunt Rachel gives David
a box full of English words to learn, and then one day
an old rocking horse appears at his door.
ISBN 0-8075-3141-3
[1. Emigration and immigration—Fiction. 2. Vocabulary—Fiction.
3. Aunts—Fiction. 4. Rocking horses—Fiction. 5. Jews—Europe—Fiction.]
I. Yardley, Joanna, ill. II. Title.

PZ7.P76955Han 1996 95-32074
[E]—dc20 CIP
AC

Published in 1996 by Albert Whitman & Company,
6340 Oakton Street, Morton Grove, Illinois 60053-2723.
Published simultaneously in Canada by
General Publishing, Limited, Toronto.

Printed in the United States of America.
10 9 8 7 6 5 4 3 2 1

To Abe Pomeranc and Max Pomeranc—
who could ask for anything more?
M.H.P.

To Dale,
my everyman.
J.Y.

Not so very long ago, a terrible war began in Europe and soon spread across oceans and continents. It was called World War II. When it finally ended, people on both sides looked around and saw how much everyone had lost. The war had killed and hurt people on both sides of the fight.

David Solomon was three years old when the fighting stopped. His family had been hiding for almost four years—hiding because they were Jewish. They'd left their home in Germany and fled from village to village, living in forests and on farms, always seeking safety, food, and shelter but finding danger and destruction instead. Now that the war was over, they wanted to move again, to a faraway place where the war had never been. They wanted to go across the ocean to America. But many other people wanted to go, too, so David and his family had to wait . . .

and wait . . .

and wait.

David waited so long that he grew three grown-up teeth and got a baby brother named Max.

And until they could leave for America, David and his family had to live in one room, which they shared with his Aunt Rachel.

And with lots and lots of words . . .

The wall beside David's bed was covered with words, each on its own piece of paper. Aunt Rachel had taught them to him one by one. David was learning a new language.

"By the time I get to New York," David said, "I want to know hundreds of English words."

So he learned the word FRIEND because Aunt Rachel said he'd make lots of new friends in America.

And BASEBALL because she said David would play baseball with all those new friends.

He learned the word TALL because she said New York was filled with tall buildings.

And STATUE because Aunt Rachel said there was a beautiful statue waiting to welcome him to America.

Soon the wall beside David's bed was a great wall of words.

hello

One afternoon, Aunt Rachel sat on the floor beside David. She pulled him very close. "I'm going to America next week," she said. "Alone."

David began to cry.

"There's only room for one of us on a Liberty ship that's leaving for New York," she said, gently drying his tears with her hand. "You know that I'll miss you every minute. But I'll work very hard to help bring you and Momma and Poppa and Max to America as soon as possible." She hugged David for a long time.

Now Aunt Rachel was crying, too.

On the day she left, Aunt Rachel gave David a green box tied with string.

"There are one hundred English words in it," she said, "ready to go up on your wall."

"I'll learn them all," David promised. He had a gift to give, too. David handed his aunt a picture of a bouquet of yellow and white flowers. Across the top, in English, he had written, "See you soon."

"Oh, something for *my* wall," said Aunt Rachel, kissing her nephew good-bye. "I love you, David."

Day after day, David learned new words from the green box. He stored them like precious jewels in his memory.

But by the time David had learned his last word—ZEBRA—his family was still waiting to leave for America. He began to think he would never see his Aunt Rachel again.

One night, David stood on his bed and took each and every word off the wall.

"My Liberty ship is never coming," he said angrily.

After that, he didn't think about America for the longest time.

Until the day everything changed . . .

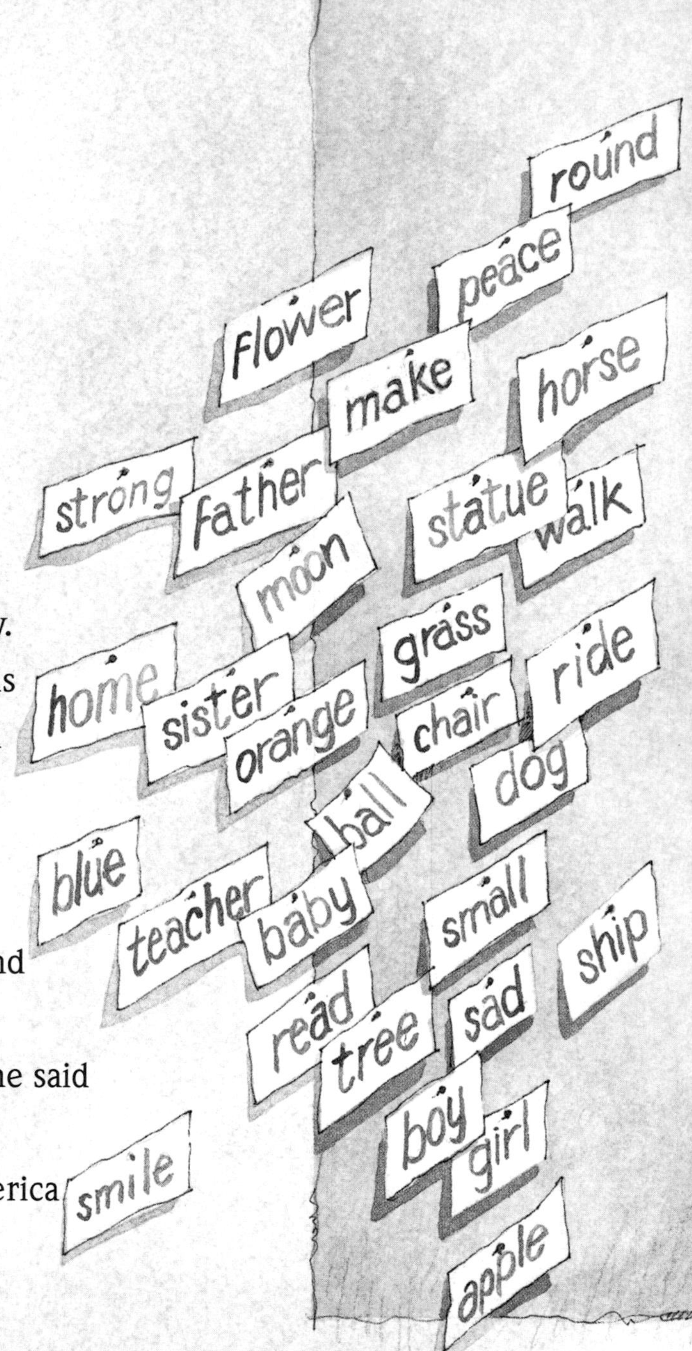

aunt
books
brother
mother
school
play
liberty
friend
tall
baseball
zebra
square
table
happy
food
light
cloud
dark

Tap-tap-tap.

"Someone's at the door," said David, running to open it. But no one was there.

"Momma, look," he whispered, without taking his eyes off what stood before him. "Momma—a horse!"

Carefully, David and his mother pulled a big old rocking horse into the room.

"Where did it come from?" David asked.

"I don't know," said his mother. "What's this?" She pointed to a yellowed note pinned to a curl on the horse's scruffy mane.

David read the note carefully.

" 'This is the Hand-Me-Down Horse. It lived with a child who just left for America. Now, if you make this special promise, it will belong to you: *WHEN I LEAVE ON MY LIBERTY SHIP, I PROMISE TO GIVE THIS ROCKING HORSE TO SOMEONE WHO IS STILL WAITING TO GO TO AMERICA.*' "

"I promise, Momma. I promise," said David, jumping onto his horse's back. "And I'm naming my horse Liberty."

David rode his rocking horse every day. He often invited Martha, who lived across the hall, to play with him. Sometimes they pretended to be soldiers, and Liberty was their tank.

"Boom, boom, boom!" shouted Martha.

Sometimes they were sea captains, and Liberty was their ship.

"Ahoy, mates," yelled David. "I see America!"

They loved riding Liberty.

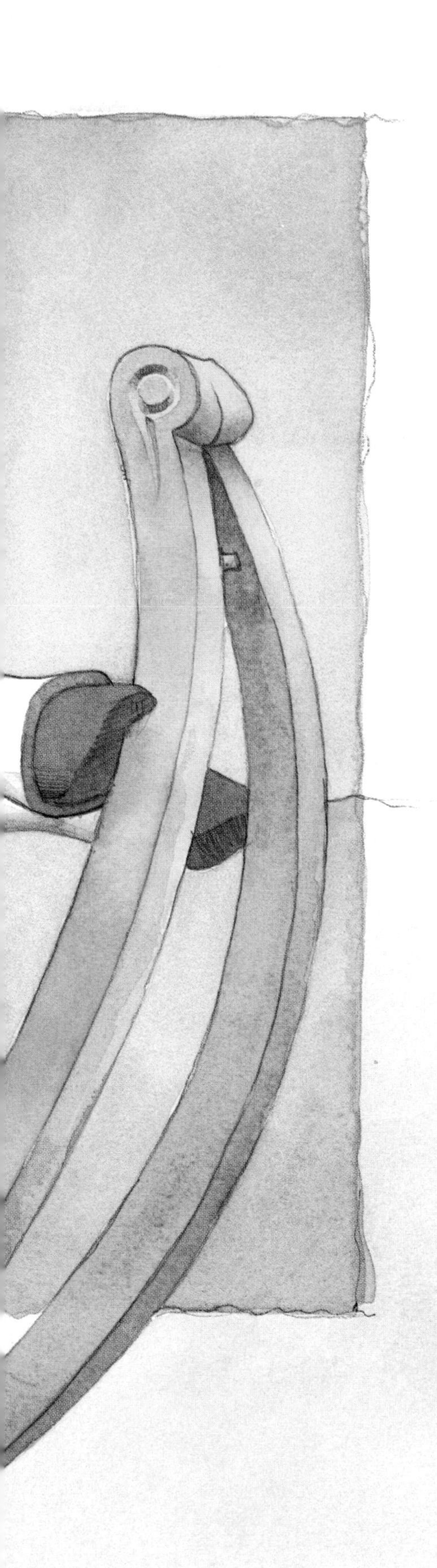

Soon David wanted to ride his horse outside. "Could we bring Liberty downstairs?" he asked one day.

David and his father carried Liberty down the stairs and across the street to a vacant lot.

"Let's put him there," said David, pointing to the only tree in sight.

That spot under the lone tree became David's favorite place to ride Liberty. As the breeze blew through his hair, David pretended to ride the Hand-Me-Down Horse across the ocean to New York City. There he saw tall buildings and children playing baseball. He saw teachers and storekeepers, policemen and mailmen. Liberty knew them all and introduced David to everyone. The best part was that David saw Aunt Rachel on each trip across the ocean.

Of course, after every visit to New York, Liberty always brought David back to the vacant lot.

One afternoon, David's parents came running across the street.

"David," called his mother. "We're leaving at last. Tomorrow!"

They had only one day to get ready before heading for their Liberty ship.

That evening the family packed and celebrated and said good-bye to their neighbors and friends. It was exciting finally to be leaving for their new home, but it was scary, too.

After everyone went to bed, David heard his mother crying late into the night.

The next morning, just before it was time to leave, David remembered the Hand-Me-Down Horse. And he remembered the special promise he had made to give Liberty to someone who was still waiting to go to America.

Only now David didn't want to.

"I wish I could squish you into a tiny ball and hide you in my pocket," David whispered to his horse. "Or take you instead of my suitcase," he added, looking at a battered brown valise.

Suddenly, *tap-tap-tap*, someone was at the door.

It was Martha. "What are you doing?" she asked.

"Getting ready for our trip," said David.

"I'm going to miss playing with you and Liberty," said Martha. "I wish I was going, too."

David looked at his friend. Then he looked at the horse.

"But Mama said we still have to wait," said Martha. "Do you think I'll ever see America?"

David took Martha's hand and parted the horse's mane.

"Liberty will help you," he said, pointing to the yellowed note that had been buried for months.

David and Martha read the note together.

"I promise," said Martha. "I really do."

Then the two children dragged the Hand-Me-Down Horse across the hall to Martha's apartment.

The Liberty ship that carried David and his family to New York was very big. And the ocean they crossed was much bigger still. Every morning David looked out over the endless gray water and wondered if New York was getting close.

One morning, after ten days at sea, he knew it was.

In the distance, standing alone on a tiny island, was the statue Aunt Rachel had told him about. The Statue of Liberty welcomed David to

America, just as she had done to thousands of other children before him.

As they pulled into the harbor, David's mother gave him something she'd been saving for a long time—the green box tied with string.

"For your wall in New York," she said.

Inside the box David found the little pieces of paper with the English words he had taken off his wall months ago.

Aunt Rachel was waiting for her family at the pier with a bouquet of yellow and white flowers.

"I'm here, Aunt Rachel," David called in English.

"Welcome to America!" Aunt Rachel called back. She was speaking English, too.

Everyone hugged and cried and talked at the same time.

Then Aunt Rachel brought David and his family to their new home. It was in a tall building that had more stairs than David had ever seen before.

And it had a wall that was perfect for his words.

Soon many new words were added to that wall.

David went to school and made new friends. Up went the words HOMEWORK, GEOMETRY and RECESS.

He went to the library and began reading American books. DETECTIVE and MYSTERY were added.

David started playing baseball, too, just like Aunt Rachel had told him he would. BUNT and KNUCKLEBALL were tacked to the wall.

He learned more and more English words, until it sounded as if he'd been speaking English for years.

One day, David was adding his latest word to the wall, when—*tap-tap-tap*—someone was at the door.

There stood a girl, smiling and happy. "Hi, David," she said. "Look, Liberty helped me, too!" Martha was in America.

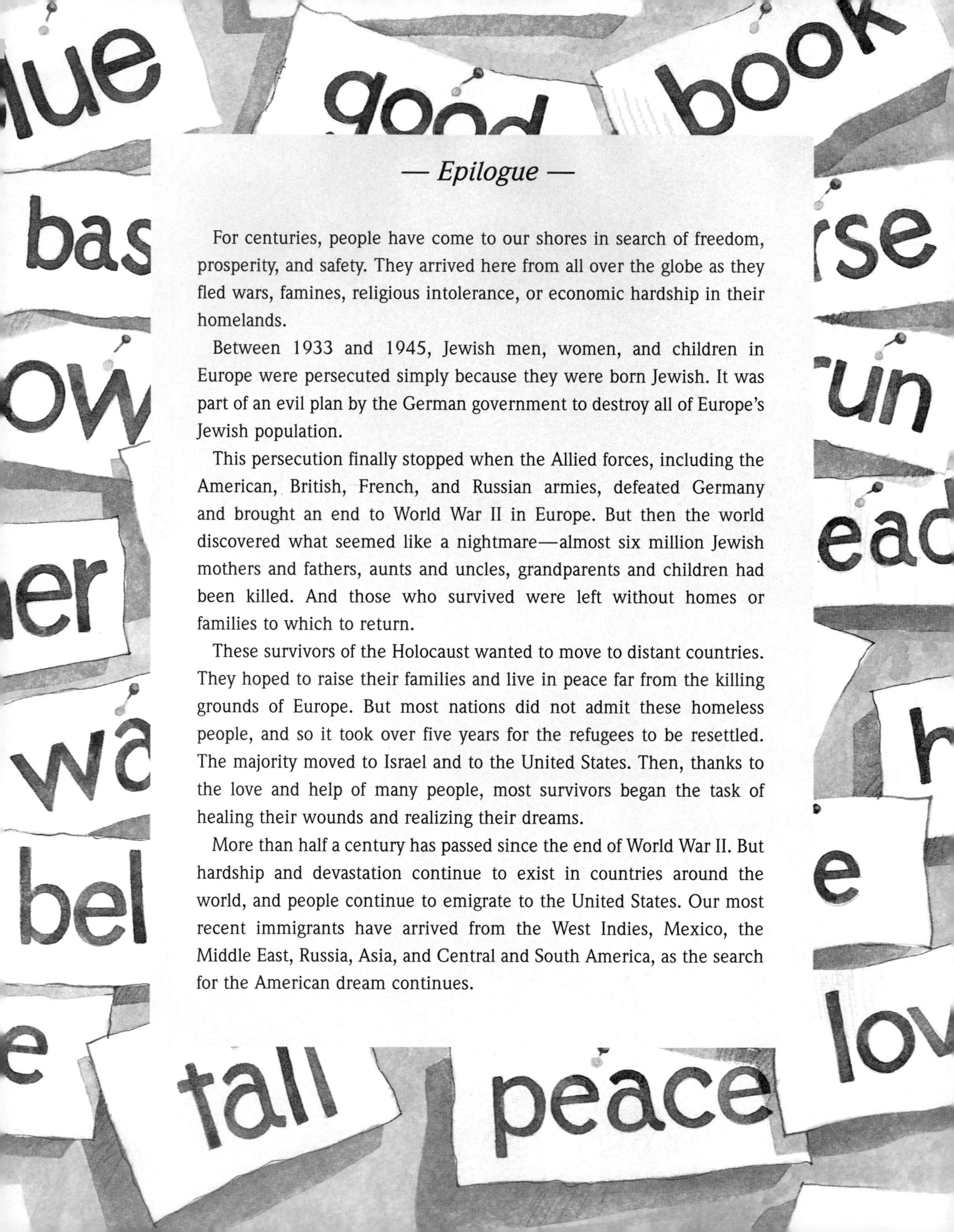

— *Epilogue* —

For centuries, people have come to our shores in search of freedom, prosperity, and safety. They arrived here from all over the globe as they fled wars, famines, religious intolerance, or economic hardship in their homelands.

Between 1933 and 1945, Jewish men, women, and children in Europe were persecuted simply because they were born Jewish. It was part of an evil plan by the German government to destroy all of Europe's Jewish population.

This persecution finally stopped when the Allied forces, including the American, British, French, and Russian armies, defeated Germany and brought an end to World War II in Europe. But then the world discovered what seemed like a nightmare—almost six million Jewish mothers and fathers, aunts and uncles, grandparents and children had been killed. And those who survived were left without homes or families to which to return.

These survivors of the Holocaust wanted to move to distant countries. They hoped to raise their families and live in peace far from the killing grounds of Europe. But most nations did not admit these homeless people, and so it took over five years for the refugees to be resettled. The majority moved to Israel and to the United States. Then, thanks to the love and help of many people, most survivors began the task of healing their wounds and realizing their dreams.

More than half a century has passed since the end of World War II. But hardship and devastation continue to exist in countries around the world, and people continue to emigrate to the United States. Our most recent immigrants have arrived from the West Indies, Mexico, the Middle East, Russia, Asia, and Central and South America, as the search for the American dream continues.